PLEASE STAND
FOR THE NATIONAL ANTHEM

PLEASE STAND
FOR THE NATIONAL ANTHEM

By Marvin Sprouse

Copyright © 2022 by Marvin Sprouse

All rights reserved. No part of this book may be reproduced in any form or by any electronic or mechanical means, including information storage and retrieval systems, without permission in writing from the publisher, except by reviewers, who may quote brief passages in a review.

ISBN: 978-1-956736-43-4 (Paperback Edition)
ISBN: 978-1-956736-44-1 (Hardcover Edition)
ISBN: 978-1-956736-42-7 (E-book Edition)

Library of Congress Control Number: 2021920454

Some characters and events in this book are fictitious. Any similarity to the real persons, living or dead, is coincidental and not intended by the author.

Book Ordering Information

Phone Number: 315 288-7939 ext. 1000 or 347-901-4920
Email: info@globalsummithouse.com
Global Summit House
www.globalsummithouse.com

Printed in the United States of America

PLEASE READ THIS IMPORTANT NOTE

This note is important because in these words I am making a promise to you, my reader. I promise that I will only write about my love of country, the men and women who have taught me that love, and I will refrain from insulting men who have been doing things I personally find offensive, (such as kneeling instead of standing during the playing of the National Anthem at NFL Games.) Unfortunately many Americans have grown in years but not necessarily in wisdom. I refuse to join my fellow citizens who are involved in name-calling and severe criticism of the men who are disrespecting our National Anthem, our flag, our country and the men and women who have so gallantly served our Nation.

Because the number of birthdays many Americans have celebrated facilitates the fact that many of them are called adults, but they grew up without the knowledge of what the name of our Country, "America," means to so many American patriots. To them the National Anthem is just another song, the American flag is just a piece of cloth and the estimated 1.1 million men and women who died for our Country simply experienced death, just as we all will someday experience death. Those people recognize the deaths of 1.1 million Americans as something stupid, something that makes absolutely no sense to them. They perceive each of those deaths as meaningless and preventable events.

God only knows how many Americans delight in cursing, complaining about and insulting our Nation and the men and women who made such magnificent sacrifices for freedom, the foundational and spiritual underpinning of our Nation. Truth was expressed so eloquently by Jefferson who wrote, "The tree of liberty must be refreshed from time to time with the blood of patriots and tyrants."

Several months ago I promised myself that I would only watch the so called News on TV for no more than 30 minutes a day. Even that meager diet is an overdose of redundancy based almost entirely on the "I-Hate-message." What many of us call "The News" has become nothing more than exercises in spewing vitriolic and hate-driven messages about people whose ideas and ideals are different from our own.

I am deeply disappointed by the disrespect so many have been showing to my National Anthem, my Flag and my Country. My purpose in writing this book is to remind any who would read these words, of the indebtedness each of us owes every last one of the men and women who gave so much so that we could remain the land of the free and the home of the brave.

DEDICATION

Most historians identify Crispus Attucks, a man who was shot dead at the Boston Masacre, by British Troops, as the first American citizen to die in the defense of his country. Citizen Attucks was an African American and an American Indian. If Crispus Attucks was the sole American to die for his country then that would be sufficient cause for me to stand with solemnity during the National Anthem, to honor his sacrifice.

Mr. Attucks was, of course, not the only American to die for his country. Here is a number I wish every person reading this book would commit to memory. That is the number frequently given as the number of men and women who gave their lives for their country. That means that I recognize 1.1 million reasons to stand in honor of my National Anthem, my Flag, my Country and those 1.1 million men and women who gave the supreme sacrifice for me, for you and for our Nation.

After extensive research I discovered that every single man or woman who gave their lives for America, every last one of them had a mother and a father. Many also had a spouse, along with a brother and or a sister. When you include the families along with the patriots who gave their all for our Nation then you have a number of at least 5.5 million people who have suffered grievously for this Country. To disrespect the established protocol of respect for the National Anthem, (Standing with the right hand covering the heart) is a gross error of good and acceptable manners and needs to be corrected immediately. Behaving with respect and honor is simply the right thing to do.

The purpose of this Book is to respectfully ask those not keeping the suggested protocols of respect, to stand up straight during the National Anthem and simply do the right thing. Every single one of us enjoys tremendous benefits from being an American Citizen, and an almost inconsequential display of respect is a small matter for each of us. God bless America and each of our remarkable citizens. Once again I ask you to please do the right thing.

TABLE OF CONTENTS

Chapter 1	Those Who Served	11
Chapter 2	The Story Of The Star Spangled Banner	35
Chapter 3	Two Brave Men	40
Chapter 4	Battlefield Miracles	48
Chapter 5	Those Who Kneel	53
Chapter 6	Are You Worthy?	59
Chapter 7	What Is Your Legacy?	62
Chapter 8	Watch Your Mouth!	66

This painting of Crispus Attucks was taken from http://wikepedia.org/wiki/Crispus-Attucks

CHAPTER ONE
THOSE WHO SERVED

"The soldier is the Army. No army is better than its soldiers. The Soldier is also a citizen. In fact, the highest obligation and privilege of citizenship is that of bearing arms for one's country"- George S. Patton Jr.

"The best way to find yourself is to lose yourself in the service of others." Mahatma Gandhi

"We will receive not what we wildly wish for but what we justly earn. Our rewards will always be in exact proportion to our service." Earl Nightingale

THOSE WHO FIGHT FOR COUNTRY

I am 80 years old and, by far, the very best men it was my privilege to meet, I met as we served the cause of our Country in Viet Nam. It is my humble opinion that those who fled to places such as Canada to avoid their obligation and responsibility to their country, were cowards and should never have been welcomed home. We would have been much better off without them.

Contrary to liberal thought, the Bible does not forbid participation in war. What the Bible does is condemn those who refuse to participate in war. Consider Jeremiah 48:10, "Cursed be he who does the work of the Lord deceitfully, and cursed is he who keeps back his sword from blood." In Luke 22:36, Jesus tells His apostles, "…he who has no sword, let him sell his garment and buy one."

Yesterday I listened to a man I respect talking on his radio program. He talked about how close we are to a civil war when political leaders talk about being violent to members of a political party they don't like. Pay attention, America, when high placed political leaders began encouraging people to practice violence you might be wise to arm yourself, and to become proficient in the use of the weapon of your choice.

In this chapter I will write about a few brave men who would do whatever it takes to defend themselves and this Nation. A few days ago I spoke with Bob Anderson. a retired Air Force Chief Master Sergeant. That is the highest enlisted rank in the Air Force. He said that people often thank him for his service. He responds that it was his privilege to serve. At the beginning of this chapter I quoted General George Patton who said that "the highest obligation and privilege of citizenship is bearing arms for one's country." I say, "Amen to that. It is indeed a great privilege to serve one's country."

JOE MARM

It was a beautiful afternoon. The First Cavalry Division had landed and taken up residence around the tiny Village of Ahn Khe in the Central Highlands of South Viet Nam. A beautiful river called the Song Bah splashed its way through the Village.On the 15th of September. 1965, the first Cavalry Division had moved in and set up a more or less permanent base camp. We renamed Ahn Khe, calling it Camp Holloway, named after a Helicopter pilot, Chief Warrant Officer. Charles Edward Holloway. On December 22, 1962, CWO Holloway, of the 81st Transportation Company. was flying South Vietnamese Soldiers (ARVN or Army of the Republic of Viet Nam) into a landing zone, near Tuy Hoa. His helicopter crashed due to enemy fire, and CWO Hollaway was killed. His body was recovered.

We had been in Viet Nam for about six weeks, just long enough to take out a few patrols, to actually become engaged in a fire fight or two, and to actually know, that regardless of what the powers that be, back in CONUS (Army-speak for the Continental Army of the United States) called our activities, we were in a real-deal shooting war. There is no way that anyone of us who lived in Camp Holloway was about to call the action we were living each day, a "police action." People on both sides were being shot, and a few Americans were going home in flag covered caskets. Captain Holloway, and a few hundred others had not died in industrial accidents. They had been killed, by a cunning group of people we called the enemy, the Viet Cong, along with their compatriots, the members of the North Vietnamese Army (NVA).

It seemed that most of the Division was on stand-down, a time which almost ceased to exist as time passed and the Division became increasingly involved in the ancient art of making war. The sides of our tents were rolled up and men sat talking on cots and in folding chairs. I led the Recon Platoon in the Second of the Fifth Battalion, led by Lieutenant Colonel Robert B. Tully. Sharing that patch of land with our Battalion, inside the confines of Camp Holloway, was the Second of the Twelfth Battalion. A few lieutenants sat around talking, smoking cigars, drinking cold beer and laughing.

Someone introduced me to a Lieutenant from the First Of the Seventh Battalion. That young Lieutenant was Joe Marm. Lieutenant Marm was wearing Kakis, his uniform decorated only by the crossed brass rifles, the insignia of an infantry officer. a gold metal bar of a Second Lieutenant, and a small cloth gold and black ranger tab sewed to the right shoulder of his uniform. We shook hands and exchanged "howdys." The entire event took less than 20 seconds. Joe Marm was a handsome young man, in the Alan Ladd tradition. He had blond hair and was deeply tanned. He had a deep voice and a mild demeanor about him. Joe could be accurately described as "mild mannered," a sort of kindness not necessarily typical of a young Army Ranger Lieutenant. My thoughts of the man I met for a few seconds were that he appeared kind, maybe too kind to lead troops in combat. I had trouble visualizing him enduring the grueling training back at the Ranger School. I would soon learn that Joe Marm had an enormous, great and extraordinary storehouse of grit, courage and masculinity.

It was less than a month later when the First of the Seventh Battalion stepped off into what would become the most violent battle of the Viet Nam War. That battle was fought in and around a bamboo covered landing zone known as Landing Zone X-ray, in an area known as the Ia Drang Valley. On the second day of that Battle, Colonel Tully's 2/5 Battalion relived Colonel Moore's 1/7 Battalion. After that and until the last man left LZ X-Ray, Colonel Tully was responsible for the defense of LZ X-Ray.

This is a transcript of an official citation describing the heroic action of Joe Marm during the Battle of the Ia Drang Valley. The action described here led to Lieutenant Marm being awarded the highest decoration of distinction in our Country, The Congressional Medal Of Honor.

Citation: For conspicuous gallantry and intrepidity at the risk of life above and beyond the call of duty. As a platoon leader in the 1st Cavalry Division (Airmobile), 1LT Marm demonstrated indomitable courage during a combat operation. His company was moving through the valley to relieve a friendly unit surrounded by an enemy force of estimated regimental size. 1LT Marm led his platoon through withering fire until they were finally forced to take cover. Realizing that his platoon could not hold very long, and seeing four enemy soldiers moving into his position, he moved quickly under heavy fire and annihilated all of them,

Then, seeing that his platoon was receiving intense fire from a concealed machine gun, he deliberately exposed himself to draw its fire. Thus locating its position, he attempted to destroy it with an antitank weapon. Although he inflicted casualties, the weapon did not silence the enemy fire. Quickly, disregarding the intense fire directed on him and his platoon, he charged 30 meters across open ground, and hurled grenades into the enemy position, killing some of the 8 insurgents manning the gun. Although severely wounded, when his grenades were expended, armed with only a rifle, he continued the momentum of his assault on the position and killed the remainder of the enemy. 1LT Marm's selfless actions reduced the fire on his platoon, broke the enemy assault, and rallied his unit to continue toward the accomplishment of this mission. 1LT Marm's gallantry on the battlefield and his extraordinary intrepidity at the risk of his life are in the highest traditions of the U.S. Army and reflect great credit upon himself and the Armed Forces of his Country.

Most men who receive medals for action such as Joe Marm performed, receive those medals posthumously. Joe was fortunate. He was severely wounded and was sent home to give his wounds time to heal. Joe Marm lived, and is still alive , traveling extensively to represent his Country, the Army and to talk about America and patriotism. As soon as his wounds healed Joe Marm volunteered to return to Viet Nam. The Army required Joe to sign papers stating that he was returning to Viet Nam because of his own choice. Thank God we have young leaders like Joe Marm in the Armed Forces today. When I read that Joe asked permission to return to Viet Nam I was reminded of the Bible verse often used to describe the commitment of missionaries. That verse is found in Isaiah 6:8, "Also I heard the voice of the Lord saying: Whom shall I send, and who will go for us?" Then I said, "Here am I, send me."

When we needed a hero one appeared in the form of Joe Marm. The things Joe did that day were extraordinary. Some would say, "impossible." Thank you, Joe Marm. Today I recall those few seconds I said hello to you and shook your hand as one of the great memories for this old man. Thanks for that memory and thanks for teaching so many young men and women what it means to be a soldier.

This photo was found at http:// www.bing.com

NO SHORTAGE OF HEROS

In the voluminous annals of the history of warfare by US Forces there is no shortage of stories about heroes, men like Joe Marm, men of remarkable courage, men who step forward when they are needed and perform far beyond the standard required of them.

In World War I, we, as a Nation, were honored by the heroic service of Sergeant Alvin C. York. Alvin Cullum York (December 13, 1887 – September 2, 1964), also known as Sergeant York, was one of the most decorated United States Army soldiers of World War I. He received the Medal of Honor, for leading an attack on a German machine-gun nest, taking at least one machine gun, killing at least 25 enemy soldiers and capturing 132. York's Medal of Honor action occurred during the United States-led portion of the Meuse-Argonne Offensive in France, which was intended to breach the Hindenberg Line and force the Germans to surrender. He earned decorations from several allied countries during WWI, including France, Italy and Montenegro. Sergeant York's fame naturally spread across the United States when a Movie was made depicting his life, in which the role of Sergeant York was played by Gary Cooper.

PLEASE STAND

This photograph of Sergeant Alvin York was taken from
https://fineartamerica.com/featured/sergeant-york-world-war-i-portrait-war-is-hell-store

AUDI MURPHY

Audi Murphy was awarded the Congressional Medal Of Honor. His Citation reads,

Lt. Audi Murphy commanded Company B, which was attacked by 6 tanks and waves of infantry. 2d Lt. Murphy ordered his men to withdraw to prepared positions in a woods, while he remained forward at his command post and continued to give fire directions to the artillery by telephone. Behind him, to his right, 1 of our tank destroyers received a direct hit and began to burn. Its crew withdrew to the woods. 2d Lt. Murphy continued to direct artillery fire which killed large numbers of the advancing enemy infantry. With the enemy tanks abreast of his position, 2d Lt. Murphy climbed on the burning tank destroyer, which was in danger of blowing up at any moment, and employed its. 50 caliber machine gun against the enemy. He was alone and exposed to German fire from 3 sides, but his deadly fire killed dozens of Germans and caused their infantry attack to waver. The enemy tanks, losing infantry support, began to fall back. For an hour the Germans tried every available weapon to eliminate 2d Lt. Murphy, but he continued to hold his position and wiped out a squad which was trying to creep up unnoticed on his right flank. Germans reached as close as 10 yards, only to be mowed down by his fire. He received a leg wound, but ignored it and continued the single-handed fight until his ammunition was exhausted. He then made his way to his company, refused medical attention, and organized the company in a counterattack which forced the Germans to withdraw. His directing of artillery fire wiped out many of the enemy; he killed or wounded about 50. 2d Lt. Murphy's indomitable courage and his refusal to give an inch of ground saved his company from possible encirclement and destruction, and enabled it to hold the woods which had been the enemy's objective.

This citation was taken from https://americanhistory.si.edu/collections/search/object/nmah_1062079

PLEASE STAND

The photo of Audi Murphy was taken from https://audiemurphy.com/photos.htm

Robert B. Tully

Robert B. Tully was born and raised in San Antonio, Texas. He graduated from West Point, and he commanded the Second of the Fifth Infantry Batallion, a unit of the First Cavalry Division, in Viet Nam and was awarded several decorations and awards, including a Silver Star. It is my humble opinion that Colonel Robert Tully was the most qualified, and the overall best Commander who ever laced up a pair of combat boots. Today the final resting place of Colonel Tully is in the Small Military Cemetery at Fort Sam Houston in San Antonio, Texas. Some of my readers will recall Colonel Tully for the time he commanded the Airborne School at Fort Benning, Georgia.

This photo of Colonel Tully was taken from

PLEASE STAND

HTTPS://WWW.GOOGLE.COM/SEARCH?Q=PHOTOS+OF+COLONEL+ROBERT+B+TULLY HYPERLINK
"HTTPS://WWW.GOOGLE.COM/SEARCH?Q=PHOTOS+OF+COLONEL+ROBERT+B+TULLY&SXSRF" HYPERLINK
"HTTPS://WWW.GOOGLE.COM/SEARCH?Q=PHOTOS+OF+COLONEL+ROBERT+B+TULLY HYPERLINK
"HTTPS://WWW.GOOGLE.COM/SEARCH?Q=PHOTOS+OF+COLONEL+ROBERT+B+TULLY&SXSRF"& HYPERLINK
"HTTPS://WWW.GOOGLE.COM/SEARCH?Q=PHOTOS+OF+COLONEL+ROBERT+B+TULLY&SXSRF"SXSRF" HYPERLINK
"HTTPS://WWW.GOOGLE.COM/SEARCH?Q=PHOTOS+OF+COLONEL+ROBERT+B+TULLY&SXSRF"& HYPERLINK
"HTTPS://WWW.GOOGLE.COM/SEARCH?Q=PHOTOS+OF+COLONEL+ROBERT+B+TULLY&SXSRF" HYPERLINK
"HTTPS://WWW.GOOGLE.COM/SEARCH?Q=PHOTOS+OF+COLONEL+ROBERT+B+TULLY HYPERLINK
"HTTPS://WWW.GOOGLE.COM/SEARCH?Q=PHOTOS+OF+COLONEL+ROBERT+B+TULLY&SXSRF"& HYPERLINK
"HTTPS://WWW.GOOGLE.COM/SEARCH?Q=PHOTOS+OF+COLONEL+ROBERT+B+TULLY&SXSRF"SXSRF" HYPERLINK
"HTTPS://WWW.GOOGLE.COM/SEARCH?Q=PHOTOS+OF+COLONEL+ROBERT+B+TULLY&SXSRF"SXSRF

This photo of a 106 Recoilless Rifle was taken from

HTTPS://WWW.GOOGLE.COM/SEARCH?SXSRF=ALEKK02VC
SFLIHLNXZFAVS2JAYHSFSBYKQ:1622442931300   HYPERLINK
"HTTPS://WWW.GOOGLE.COM/SEARCH?SXSRF=ALEKK02VCSFLIH
LNXZFAVS2JAYHSFSBYKQ:1622442931300&SOURCE=UNIV&TBM=I
SCH&Q=PHOTO+OF+106+RECOILLESS+RIFLE&SA"&   HYPERLINK
"HTTPS://WWW.GOOGLE.COM/SEARCH?SXSRF=ALEKK02VCSFLIHLNX
ZFAVS2JAYHSFSBYKQ:1622442931300&SOURCE=UNIV&TBM=ISCH&Q=
PHOTO+OF+106+RECOILLESS+RIFLE&SA"SOURCE=UNIV   HYPERLINK
"HTTPS://WWW.GOOGLE.COM/SEARCH?SXSRF=ALEKK02VCSFLIH
LNXZFAVS2JAYHSFSBYKQ:1622442931300&SOURCE=UNIV&TBM=I
SCH&Q=PHOTO+OF+106+RECOILLESS+RIFLE&SA"&   HYPERLINK
"HTTPS://WWW.GOOGLE.COM/SEARCH?SXSRF=ALEKK02VCSFLIHLN
XZFAVS2JAYHSFSBYKQ:1622442931300&SOURCE=UNIV&TBM=ISCH&
Q=PHOTO+OF+106+RECOILLESS+RIFLE&SA"TBM=ISCH   HYPERLINK
"HTTPS://WWW.GOOGLE.COM/SEARCH?SXSRF=ALEKK02VCSFLIH
LNXZFAVS2JAYHSFSBYKQ:1622442931300&SOURCE=UNIV&TBM=I
SCH&Q=PHOTO+OF+106+RECOILLESS+RIFLE&SA"&   HYPERLINK
"HTTPS://WWW.GOOGLE.COM/SEARCH?SXSRF=ALEKK02VCSFLIHLNX
ZFAVS2JAYHSFSBYKQ:1622442931300&SOURCE=UNIV&TBM=ISCH&Q=P
HOTO+OF+106+RECOILLESS+RIFLE&SA"Q=PHOTO+OF+106+RECOILLES
S+RIFLE   HYPERLINK   "HTTPS://WWW.GOOGLE.COM/SEARCH?SXSRF=AL
EKK02VCSFLIHLNXZFAVS2JAYHSFSBYKQ:1622442931300&SOURCE=UNIV
&TBM=ISCH&Q=PHOTO+OF+106+RECOILLESS+RIFLE&SA"&   HYPERLINK
"HTTPS://WWW.GOOGLE.COM/SEARCH?SXSRF=ALEKK02VCS
FLIHLNXZFAVS2JAYHSFSBYKQ:1622442931300&SOURCE=UNIV
&TBM=ISCH&Q=PHOTO+OF+106+RECOILLESS+RIFLE&SA"SA

PLEASE STAND

HTTPS://WWW.GOOGLE.COM/SEARCH?Q=PHOTOS+FROM+FUNERAL+OF+COLONEL+ROBERT+B+TULLY HYPERLINK "HTTPS://WWW.GOOGLE.COM/SEARCH?Q=PHOTOS+FROM+FUNERAL+OF+COLONEL+ROBERT+B+TULLY&SXSRF"& HYPERLINK "HTTPS://WWW.GOOGLE.COM/SEARCH?Q=PHOTOS+FROM+FUNERAL+OF+COLONEL+ROBERT+B+TULLY&SXSRF" SXSRF

Colonel Tully was a devout Catholic. We had a Chaplain assigned to our Battalion who had signed up as a United States Army Chaplain in his homeland of Italy. Every morning our Chaplain would wake up early and make his way over to the tent we had designated as our church. He celebrated a Mass early each day. Often he celebrated the mass for only one lone worshiper. Often Colonel Tully knelt alone in our church tent to celebrate the mass with our Chaplain. It was somehow reassuring to know that our Commander talked to God every morning.

Colonel Tully was a complex gentleman, and it is not possible to describe the essence of the man in a few paragraphs. I will now submit two stories about Robert B. Tully that I believe will give you at least a glimmer of light about the man he was.

The first incident describes an early morning event. Colonel Tully was sitting in his jeep with his driver on a small bridge that crossed a shallow creek. About ten yards away from Colonel Tully's jeep was another jeep carrying a 106 Recoilless rifle and it's crew. Calling that weapon a rifle is probably misleading to most people, because it looks much more like a cannon than a rifle. The Lieutenant leading the 106 Rifle Platoon was in the jeep with his driver and another crew member. The weapon was loaded and Colonel Tully and the crew of the 106 Recoilless Rifle were out looking for targets. It was Colonel Tully who spotted the first target of the day. About a half a mile away, a lone man, wearing black pajamas was walking leisurely across a rice paddy. That area had been cleared the previous day and Colonel Tully knew that anyone in that area was an enemy, a Viet Cong.

When Colonel Tully saw the man in the black pajamas he called out, "There. Shoot that guy."

Seconds later there was a loud bang, as the 50 Caliber Spotting rifle, mounted securely to the Barrel of the 106 Recoilless

Rifle, fired, and sent a bullet flying toward the man in the black pajamas. The round hit about two feet from the man. It exploded, as it is designed to do, sending a small white cloud into the sky.

The purpose of the 50 caliber spotting rife is to tell the crew exactly where the much bigger 106 shell would hit. They fired the big gun and a second later, the 106 round hit precisely where the fifty caliber spotting round had impacted. Incredibly the 106 round was a dud, and it went skipping across the rice paddy like a flat rock tossed out onto a pond.

The gun crew was moving very quickly, just as they had been trained to do. They were loading another 106 round and preparing to fire another round.

It was at that exact moment that Colonel Tully intervened, He said, "Wait! Don't shoot." Then he added, "That lucky rascal deserves to live."

So it happened that the man in the black pajamas lived another day. He was running very fast and who knows if he is still running today? At the rate he was running he might have run out of Viet Nam, across China and half way across Russia. He was indeed a lucky rascal, and he did indeed deserve to live.

The next story I want to tell you about Colonel Tully occurred on a bright and sunny afternoon. It was about a week since we had fought in the Battle of the Ia Drang Valley at LZ X-ray The men were enjoying that rare event, an afternoon of down time. The men sat in small groups telling stories, or taking naps on inflated air mattresses.

Suddenly the solitude of the afternoon was shattered when a Specialist who worked in the Command Tent came running into our area. He was yelling, "Lieutenant Sprouse. Has anyone seen Lieutenant Sprouse?"

"Hey, I'm here," I called out to him.

 The young man stopped running, and he was clearly out of breath, "He said, "Colonel Tully wants to see you at the C.P., right away." Then he added, "He said to bring all your gear. "

I grabbed my gear, and my M-16 rifle and took off running for the C.P. When I got there Colonel Tully was standing outside with a map in his hand. He immediately began to brief me.

"In five minutes six choppers will land in that field," He said, pointing to a grassy field about 100 yards from where we were standing.

"Load up your platoon," he continued, "and fly out four clicks to this location." He said, pointing to a blue circle he had drawn on his map. "Dig in for the night and just see if you can hear or see anything." By that time my Platoon Sergeant, Sergeant Roy Salinas, was standing by and listening along with me.

A few minutes later our platoon was loaded on the Choppers and flying, on a very short flight, toward our objective. We had two special men with us. One was an artillery observer, and he could call in heavy artillery (105 Artillery rounds) any place we wanted them. The other man was an Air Force Lieutenant, and he could call in an air stroke any place we wanted it.

We landed quickly with no apparent enemy in sight and began to prepare our positions for the long night ahead. In the Recon Platoon every Squad has a PRC-25 Radio. The Radios were all turned on and the loud speakers on each of them sent out the next messages.

It was Colonel Tully's voice and he was speaking with a lot of calm and obvious control of the communication. He said. "As those choppers were flying out they went to your North. They spotted a force of about 500 North Vietnamese Soldiers. They are about a click from you and they are headed your way. The Choppers need to refuel and it will be dark soon, so they can't help you."

Colonel Tully then talked me through the procedures for preparing for an overnight defensive position. I had already gone through all of those procedures dozens of times since we had arrived in Viet Nam. I began by having the Artillery Non Commissioned Officer assigned to our platoon do his thing. He got on the radio to an Artillery Company from our Division Artillery Batallion. He registered an artillery round, having the Artillery Company actually fire a round into a nearby field. That field was what we had determined was the most likely avenue of approach for the enemy force which had been spotted.

Then my Battalion Commander had me deploy the Platoon's two M-60 machine guns preparing to fire in the direction we believed the most likely approaches to our position. As we talked my men were digging in, preparing foxholes in a perimeter we were preparing to defend. As the men worked quickly, they continued to hear the voice of our Commander.

Keep in mind that we were preparing, with 33 men to defend our position against 500 enemy soldiers. That is about twice as many men as the manuals all claim to be a force sufficient to overrun a dug-in force. What the manuals did not consider was that we had both 105 Artillery and airplanes loaded with both high ordinance and napalm bombs. Soon we were ready for the night. We had placed Claymore mines around our perimeter, and we were all dug in. Waiting and ready.

I noticed that as the men worked, they were all paying close attention to the voice of Colonel Tully, which they could all hear clearly over the radios. I would, incredibly, describe the mood of the men in our Platoon as jubilant. We were, in fact, preparing for an assault by a force which greatly outnumbered us. The men were laughing, joking, and high fiving one another. You would have thought they were anticipating a picnic instead of an attack by a much greater force than our own.

I believe that hearing our Commander's voice inspired confidence in those men and caused their happy and confident moods. They were as impressed by the sound of the Colonel's calm and confident voice as they were with the actual words he was communicating. I believe that for many of those men, Colonel Tully's voice sounded like a father, a leader who not only wanted to make sure our preperations were complete, but the voice of the fathers many of those men had never experienced.

Not long ago, just a month before Colonel Tully died, at the age of 93, I enjoyed a phone conversation with him. I asked if he remembered the day we prepared to meet the five hundred enemy soldiers. He said, "Oh, yes, I think about that day often." And then he added, "You know, Marvin, I think you guys could have handled them."

That was an amazing thing for me to hear. After more than 50 years, my Commander still remembered me, and he still had a lot of confidence in me and the platoon I led. I was deeply honored.

SOME OTHER HEROES OF MINE

Not all the heroes I know who gave their all for their country needed to do that in the face of an armed enemy. Some men work with danger in their jobs simply because of the way they serve their beloved country. One such man was a helicopter pilot named Charles William Thigpen III, a helicopter pilot whose last assignment was at the Humboldt Bay Coast Guard Station at Eureka, California. A distress call came in one afternoon telling about a group of Canadians who were stranded in a small boat about fifty miles off the coast of California. The pilot scheduled to fly a rescue mission that afternoon, for some reason, was not available to fly, so Charles William Thigpen III flew the mission. They found the vessel and were lowering a rescue cage to pick up survivors. Suddenly a rogue wave appeared and sent a finger of water an amazing sixty feet into the air. The wave seized the rear propellers of the helicopter and they stopped turning. Onlookers reported that from the time the propellers stopped turning until the vessel disappeared beneath the dark waters of the Pacific took an elapsed time of five seconds. Thus Charles William Thigpen gave his life while serving his country in the United States Coast Guard, Thank you, Officer Thigpen. You are remembered by your neice, Laura Powell, of Birmingham, Alabama, who heard that I was writing this book and wanted me to include your story on these pages. Thank you, sir, for your service. May you be remembered.

LEST WE FORGET THE WOMEN WHO SERVED SO WELL

This photo of Colonel McSally was taken from //www.bing.com/images/search?q=photos+of+co lonel+martha+mcsally&qpvt=photos+of+colonel+matha+mcsally&form=IGRE&first=1&tsc=Ima geBasicHover

Martha Elizabeth McSally (born March 22, 1966) is an American politician who served as the Congresswoman for Arizona's 2nd congressional district. A retired military officer, McSally served in the United States Air Force from 1988 to 2010 and rose to the rank of Colonel. One of the highest-ranking female pilots in the history of the Air Force, McSally was the first American woman to fly in combat following the 1991 lifting of the prohibition on female combat pilots.

Colonel McSally flew the Fairchild Republic A-10 Thunderbolt II close air support aircraft over Iraq and Kuwait during Operation Southern Watch. McSally was also the first female commander of a USAF fighter squadron (the FS), based near Tucson, Arizona.

PLEASE STAND

I recently heard Colonel McSally talking about having been raped by a senior Air Force Officer. Please note that I did not refer to this dirt bag of a human being as a "Superior" Officer. I obviously have no experience in having been raped. I do wish that Colonel McSally had come forward soon enough to have that sorry rascal eliminated from the Corps of Officers who so proudly serve their country. I have no experience in such matters and have no inkling of why Colonel McSallly concealed the identity of her attacker for so long. I can't even imagine the personal anguish of a woman who has been mistreated like that.

Senator Martha Elizabeth McSally, a Republican, served as a Senator from the 2nd Congressional District of Arizona from 2019 till 2020. At least she can address an audience without hearing a chant of "Lock her up!"

THE LAST MAN ON MY LIST OF HEROES- BUT CERTAINLY NOT THE LEAST

The last man on my list of personal heroes is my Dad, Marvin "Cotton" Sprouse Sr. During the 1020's Dad played shortstop for a semi-pro baseball team in Buffalo, South Carolina. By the time he was 21, Dad had a head of snow white hair. That hair earned him the nickname of "Cotton" Sprouse. Dad had gotten "The Call," the call every semi-pro baseball player prays he will receive one day. Dad had been called to ride the train to St. Louis, and try out for the big league team in that city. On the very day Dad was scheduled to get on that train and take that long ride to St. Louis, something terrible happened. A local woman shot Dad with a pistol. He had surgery on his left arm, and the surgeon inserted a wire into his arm, After that surgery, Dad could not straighten his arm out all the way. That is , of course, unacceptable for a major league shortstop. On the day he was shot, Dad's beautiful dream of becoming a major league shortstop died. End of that story.

This all might sound vaguely familiar to those of you who saw the Movie titled "The Natural," where Robert Redford portrayed a baseball player who gets shot by a woman on the very day he is scheduled to report to the Majors for his shot at glory. In the Movie the player who gets shot does recover completely, and does get his magnificent time at bat. That is the way things work with fiction; things can and often do all work out for the good of the hero. With my Dad, there was no chance of a come-back, not ever. Dad got shot and that ended that. As a refrain from an old Johnny Cash song tells us,"I don't like it but I guess things happen that way."

It was fifty years after Dad's Baseball career ended when he took me back to the tiny town of Lockhart, South Carolina, where he had been raised. We both needed haircuts so we both walked the two blocks to the Barber Shop. It seemed like everything in Lockhart was two blocks away.

The two barbers in that shop carried on as if Dad had a name like Ruth, Mays or Dimaggio. After things died down a bit two customers came in and they started going on and on about what a ball player ole "Cotton" had been. I soon caught on that I was in the company of a real-deal South Carolina Celebrity; my very own Dad, ole "Cotton" Sprouse.

Dad, of course wanted me to play baseball, but I was too clumsy for that. I could hit a ball and put that succor into orbit, but I couldn't catch anything, and throwing the ball was always out of my paygrade.

One night I hit a softball and believed it was going over the centerfield fence. That didn't happen, and the ball bounced off the fence and back out onto the field. I took off running. I touched first base and then I stepped on second base before lighting out for third base. As soon as I was headed for third base I saw my problem. A tall, skinny kid was blocking my path to third base, and he was standing there holding the ball, waiting to tag me out.

I would like to convince you that I had no intention of harming that skinny third baseman. If, however, you had seen what happened next you would probably never believe that. Not in a billion years.

Not only was I extraordinarily clumsy, but I knew about as much about the finesse of the game of softball as I knew about Nuclear Physics. I had absolutely nothing in my heart or on my mind about doing harm to the third baseman. I just wanted him to get out of my way so I could land on third base.

I was several yards from the third baseman when I did what I had seen Superman do on TV dozens of times; I started flying. I was flying through the air, feet first, with both legs cocked. When I came into contact with the skinny kid I kicked out with both legs, and sent that kid, wih both arms flying around in circles, as he went stumbling backwards toward the dugout. He made it all the way to the dugout, and I came down hard on third base.

The field where we were playing belonged to Saint Joseph's Catholic Church in Ensley, Alabama. St. Joseph's Church was also home to three Trinitarian Brothers, Bother Valarian, Brother Cosmus and Brother Christopher. Those brothers were sort of like coaches, and sort of like cops. They were there to keep the peace, in a steel working town like Ensley, which is part of Birmingham, and juts right up against the United States Steel Mill. The most imposing of the three Trinitarians was brother Christopher, who was just a bit taller than, and a bit better looking than Rock Hudson.

As soon as I kicked the skinny kid into the dugout, his Dad became very angry and got very involved in the whole thing. He had just seen what probably looked to him like me trying to commit homicide on his son on third base. The third baseman's Dad was about six foot four, and wearing a green softball uniform. In a flash he was on the field, yanking me up and into the air.

Then, out of absolutely nowhere my Dad arrived on the scene and he was wailing on Mr. Six Foot Four in the green softball uniform. That was an amazing thing to see because my Dad was about five feet, nine inches tall, and maybe not even that tall. Thanks Dad. I am still very, very proud to have had you for my Dad. We'll have a lot to talk about when I get to heaven, and I want to apologize to that third baseman and to Mr. Green Softball Uniform.

CHAPTER TWO
THE STORY OF THE STAR SPANGLED BANNER

"The Olympic Gold medal in 1968 was definitely the highest moment of my career. It was a dream come true. I was a 19-year-old boy, and it was just amazing to be standing on top of the podium and hearing the National Anthem in the background." George Foreman

"And you know, being able to wear the stars and stripes, when you step up on one of those blocks or, you know, when you step off an airplane or when you hear the National Anthem play, you know, its one of the greatest feelings in the world because you know that there are people at home who are supporting you and watching you." Michael Phelps

"I can't claim to know all the words of all the national anthems in the world, but I don't know of any other that ends with a question and a challenge as ours does. Does that flag still wave o'er the land of the free and the home of the brave? That is what we must all ask" Ronald Reagan

I have an intense love of history. I especially enjoy going to the exact spots where history was made and standing where those men who made that history stood as history unfolded for them.

I must have walked fifty miles exploring London. I, of course, saw what all the tourists saw; the tower of London, London Bridge, Big Ben, and Number 10 Downing Street. One thing stood out for me. That lingering memory I still have today is of what the British people called "the stake," as in "Burning someone at the stake."

What is simply called the stake is a pole covered with shiny black metal, rising from a cobblestone walkway. The stake is about 10 inches thick and shoots up about five feet high. Men who could not or would not live in compliance with the dictates of the Government, and more specifically, The Church of England, were frequently executed by being burned at that stake. I looked at that post and imagined peons running about stacking limbs and logs around the men or women to be burned. Then I imagined two soldiers carrying large lighted torches out to the pile of wood surrounding the prisoners who were tied securely to the stake, and lighting that wood.

That kind of enforcement sort of inspires one to be religious, to be very precisely religious as dictated by the great and powerful Church of England. When I think of that kind of "piety," of subjects fearing for their very lives and rigidly living out the dictates of "their church," it's easy to understand why hundreds of British subjects went sneaking down the backstreets of London, to board ships sailing for some vaguely defined place called "The new world." No wonder those ships were packed with subjects who had had their fill of cruelty and terror used to impose the dictates of the so called "Church" and the House of Parliament. I saw all of those things in my mind.

To have any appreciation at all of who those so called Colonists were is to never forget that every last one of them was a refugee seeking nothing more complicated that the fundamental right to worship as each of them saw fit.

The British would have been much more swift in "attending to" those colonists in America had it not been for the major annoyance in Europe of a short, fat Frenchman named Napoleon

Bonaparte. Lord Wellington, upon a great field called Waterloo attended to the Frenchman and that left time for the British to turn their attention back to those annoying heretics across the Atlantic.

The British showed up ready to rumble and their first stop was Washington, where they destroyed the President's home, The Capital and the Treasury building. The British were feeling pretty confident after they made a mess in Washington. Next, they headed for the third largest city in the New Land, Baltimore. Vice Admiral Cochrane commanded a fleet of `19 ships, along with a ground force of 5,000 men, and his intention was to knock out Fort McHenry. Understand what a crucial target Fort McHenry was. If the British could destroy the Fort and the troops at the Fort, they could not only have access to Baltimore, but they could move down the eastern coast destroying every colony in their path and thus conquering the new land.

The British had two Americans on board as they began their 25 hour bombardment of Fort McHenry. Francis Scott Key, a 36 year old Lawyer and amateur poet, had rowed out to the ship, The Minden, under a white flag, to negotiate the release of a personal friend of his , Dr. William Beans. Dr Beans was a Scotsman, and he spoke with a heavy Scottish brogue throughout his life.

When the bombardment of Fort McHenry began the British Captain required Mr. Key and Dr. Beans to stay on board the Minden, because they had been his guests at supper, and he knew they had heard him speaking with his men about their military plans and intentions. The Fort was bombarded through the night, for 25 hours without ceasing. It was estimated that during the 25 hour bombardment of Fort McHenry, the British fired 133 tons of ordinance.

When the dawn came there was thick fog blocking the view of the Fort from the harbor. Finally there was a brief break in the fog and Frances Scott Key felt elated to look through that clear sky and see that the American flag was still flying above Fort McHenry. Quickly the amateur poet took out his pencil along with an envelope containing a letter. In a few minutes, he wrote a five stanza poem about the survival of that flag.

The Commanding Officer of Fort McHenry, Major George Armistead, who was promoted to the rank of Lieutenant Colonel a few days after the Battle for Fort McHenry, had commissioned a local seamstress to make two flags. One flag was to be huge and the other, called a "Storm Flag," was to be used during inclement weather. Some historians hold that the storm flag flew over Fort McHenry during the bombardment and that the main flag replaced it the next morning.

Available documentation shows that the main flag was sewn by local flagmaker Mary Young HYPERLINK "https://en.wikipedia.org/wiki/Mary_Young_Pickersgill" HYPERLINK "https://en.wikipedia.org/wiki/Mary_Young_Pickersgill" under a government commission in 1813 at a cost of $405.90 (equivalent to $5,147 in 2017). George Armistead, the commander of Fort McHenry, specified in his instructions to the seamstress that he wanted, "a flag so large that the British would have no difficulty seeing it from a distance". The Flag contained 15 stars and 15 stripes. The flag now displayed at the Smithsonian in Washington, has only 14 stars. Some contend that one star was removed and sent to President Lincoln. Others argue that the star was buried with a veteran of the Battle for Fort McHenry.

The Star-Spangled Banner" was recognized for official use by the United States Navy in 1889, and by U.S. president Woodrow Wilson in 1916, and was made the national anthem by a congressional resolution on March 3, 1931

The staff of the Smithsonian could be seen for months working on the flag which was maintained under glass. If you go to the Smithsonian today to see the Star Spangled Banner, you can note that care was taken to maintain the holes in the flag and the smudges of dirt and blood, causing the flag to appear as it must have on that morning after the original bombardment.

Frances Scott Key, published the poem he had written, in a pamphlet titled the Bombardment of Fort Mc Henry. The first complimentary copies went to the men who manned the Fort during the bombardment. The pamphlet then was sold widely as many Americans read the story behind The Star Spangled Banner. Frances Scott Key died of pleurisy in 1843.

CHAPTER THREE
Two Brave Men

"You are one of a kind, one in a billion, an incredible unique individual. The problem is, so is everybody else." Deacon Jones

"We sleep peaceably in our beds at night only because rough men stand ready to do violence on our behalf."-. George Orwell.

"Nobody who ever gave his best regretted it." George Halas, former head coach of the Chicago bears.

"If it doesn't matter who wins or loses then why do they keep score?" Vince Lombardi

In this Chapter I will present slices from the lives of two men. Neither man is real. I fictionalized each of them to illustrate the main points of this Book. One man, Bobby Don Malone from Red Dirt, Alabama, is a Specialist Fourth Class serving with the Army in Afghanistan and making $23,000 a year. The other man, Ted Boudreaux, from Baton Rouge, is a defensive back playing for an NFL Team and making 3 million dollars a year.

BOUDRY SEES THE TIP-OFF

They called him Boudry, but his real name was Theodore Boudreaux. Boudry played Cornerback for the Dallas Cowboys. One bright Sunday afternoon, the Cowboys were hosting the New York Jets at Cowboy Stadium in Dallas. Boudry watched closely as the Jets broke their huddle and came up to the Line of Scrimmage. He was paying particular attention to the man wearing the Jets number 88 Jersey, Frank Bradon. Just before Frank Bradon got down in his stance, Boudry saw him glance at the pylon in the far corner of the field, where the goal line intersects with the sideline. That glance only lasted for an instant, but Boudry also noticed that the glance came with a grin on Mr. Bradon's face.

Okay sucker. I know where you are headed," thought Theodore Boudreaux. The ball was snapped, and Frank Bradon took off, running not for the corner at the far end of the field, but on a slant pattern for the closest sideline.

Boudry hung back and just watched. After the Jets, number 88 had taken precisely 6 steps, Frank Bradon planted his right foot hard, pivoted, and took off for the far corner of the field. Again, Boudry held back, not wanting to alert Jasper Frederickson, the Jets Quarterback, that he was close enough to the Jets player wearing Jets Jersey number 88, to intercept the ball. Jasper Frederickson planted his foot, cocked his arm and threw the football.

The ball launched in a high spiral, sailing toward the far corner of the field. Now that the quarterback had committed himself, Boudry took off, running as fast as his legs would push him, as he pursued Frank Bradon headed for the far corner of the field.

Boudry allowed himself a quick backwards glance when he was five yards from the corner of the field. He caught a glimpse of the football, slowly descending from its spiraling flight, and coming down into the outstretched arms of Frank Bradon.

Boudry pushed his right foot down hard and went leaping as high as he possibly could into the Dallas afternoon sky. As he jumped, he shot his arm into the sky as far as he could. He only managed to touch the ball with the tips of two fingers. When he did make that tenuous contact with the ball, he gave the ball a tiny push.

Immediately the football broke out of that smooth spiraling flight and started abruptly to drop, down toward the green turf of the Dallas field. Boudry smiled as he thrust forward both arms and snatched the falling football out of the air.

Boudry tucked the ball into the crook of his arm and spun around, and then he began running as fast as he possibly could for the far end of the field, now a distant 97 yards away.

Boudry then bowed his head and ran over a Jets player he knew was named Jerry Bates. He watched as Mr. Bates fell to earth hard.

Later, Boudry would enjoy watching the high-lights film. It looked to him like every citizen of New York was wearing a green Jersey and chasing him down the sideline, He especially enjoyed that film because it clearly showed that Boudry, with every two or three strides, was gaining a step in his escape up that sideline. That film would help Boudry's agent negotiate for more money for him during the next season. After Boudry crossed midfield, he allowed himself a quick glance at the rest of the field. The only thing between Boudry and the end zone was a Jets player wearing number 45.

Boudry didn't know number 45's name. Boudry was surprised that he didn't recognize number 45. An important part of his study assignment had been to be able to recognize each of those men in green jerseys who came to Dallas for the sole purpose of humiliating anyone wearing a Cowboy Uniform. Boudry switched the ball to his outside arm and got ready to fire his best stiff arm move at number 45.

Boudry was now right in front of number 45, and he shot his arm out, slamming his hand into the helmet of the man who wanted to stop him, and possibly to murder him.. Later he would realize that he had broken his finger and wrist when he stiff armed

PLEASE STAND

number 45. He watched as number 45 fell clumsily away from him and out of his path into the end zone. Seconds later Boudry crossed the goal line and circled around the end zone to slow down. He noticed that everywhere he looked he saw camera men and women with ridiculously long lenses, taking his picture.

The Fourth Quarter passed like part of a very sweet dream. The Cowboys won that game by a score of 17-12. Boudry would always think of that afternoon as his day in Dallas.

Boudry went into the Locker room enjoying every one of the pats on his back and his bottom, and very happy to be alive for that particular afternoon.

After his shower Boudry slipped into his six thousand dollar suit. Then he pulled on the pair of custom made boots the old man in San Antonio had made for him for only four thousand dollars. Finally, he slipped on the full length sable coat that he had picked up for only 22 thousand dollars.

A minute or two later Boudry was out in the Dallas evening. Seeing his chauffer standing, holding the back door to his Hummer Limo open for him brought a huge smile to his face. He grinned, took a last wave to a couple of hundred adoring fans and stepped down into his limo.

When the limo pulled up in front of the Hyatt Regency Hotel ten minutes later, there were about a hundred men and women there to applaud for him as he stepped out of the limo and walked into the Hotel.

Boudry walked past a young woman who took his Stetson cowboy hat and his luxurious fur coat. About two minutes later Boudry saw a beautiful blond haired woman he had long admired, walk up to him wearing his fur coat. She quickly let him see that all she had on was his coat and her high heeled shoes. The woman took Boudry's hand and led him to the elevators in the hallway. The couple then got off the elevators on the top floor and walked into a lavishly appointed room where Boudry would enjoy the most exciting sexual liaison of his lifetime. Boudry partied all through the night and into the next morning, before falling into a sweet and blissful sleep

PLEASE STAND

This photo of the Welcome to Camp Leatherneck sign was taken from q=camp+leatherneck+in+afghanistan&qpvt=Camp+Leatherneck+in+Afghanistan&form=IGRE&first=1&tsc=ImageBasicHover

BOBBY DON MALONE

Bobby Don Malone was the son of Ben Lawrence Malone, a poultry Farmer from Red Dirt, Alabama. He enlisted in the Marine Corps, and as soon as the powers that be in the Corps saw how accurate he was on the rifle range, they pulled him from the ranks and sent him off for special training as a Marine Corps Sniper.

Corporal Bobby Don Malone was given a special assignment as a sniper, assigned to a Marine Corps Unit, stationed at Camp Leatherneck, a special 1600 acre base for Marines in the southwest corner of Afghanistan, in Helmand Province. Bobby Don slept in the last tent in a long row of tents. His tent was reserved for Marine Corps snipers and a few special ops Marines.

It was an ordinary day at Camp Leatherneck, hot and sunny even early in the morning. Bobby Don got up, dressed and left for his daily walk. He walked a route that took him down to the rifle range, and then back through the living quarters on the base, a route of five and a half miles. Bobby Don enjoyed the solitude of his walks. Back home he had also taken a lot of long walks. Around Red Dirt it was best to walk, not jog or run, in case you should disturb some sleeping serpent on one of the many dirt roads that ran through the swamp in and around Red Dirt, Alabama.

When Bobby Don came to fourth street he turned North. He was looking at the hills about half a click past the fence of the camp when he saw something flash. The sun light was bouncing off a piece of glass or something shiny enough to catch the sun's reflection. A couple of seconds later he heard a shot and saw a small flicker of flame from what he knew was a firing rifle or pistol. Bobby Don wondered if that round had been fired at him. A fact popped into his head and that fact concerned the velocity of a 30 caliber round fired from an M-1 rifle, one of the most frequently used sniper rifles in the world. He recalled effortlessly

PLEASE STAND

that the velocity of a 30 caliber round was 2800 feet per second. Unfortunately, that was the very last thought ever to enter the mind of Corporal Bobby Don Malone. "2800 feet per second," he thought as the bullet struck him just above his left eye. His knees buckled, and he fell dead in the street. The sniper who had killed Bobby Don lept up on a waiting horse and galloped off down a trail. In a quarter of a mile, he dismounted, and led his horse into a large cave. Already he could hear a helicopter, flying overhead, investigating the shot he had taken.

Six Days later, Bobby Don's father, Ben Lawrence Malone was raking out one of the five long hen houses on his poultry farm. He heard the sedan pulling up in front of his house. He felt faint, knowing exactly who the two men in that sedan were and why they had come to find him that morning.

Ben Lawarence threw down his rake and began running for the house. He wanted to beat his wife Martha, to the front door. He knew that she, just as he had done, would immediately recognize the two men in Marine Corps Uniforms. Yes, she would immediately know who they were and why they had come to Malone's Poultry Farm that morning.

Those men were approaching the front door to the Malone home in Red Dirt, Alabama with the worst news a Father or a Mother could possibly hear. They were knocking on the door to tell the Malone's that Bobby Don was dead, and that he would be coming back home in a flag-draped casket.

Buck and Wanda Stemmons, who managed the Red Dirt Memorial Cemetrary, called the 17 people who attended Bobby Don Malone's funeral, as "a good crowd,", and by Red Dirt standards it was that indeed. Two Marines showed up and made a presentation of the flag that had draped Bobby Don's casket, to Mrs. Malone. Bobby Don had lived a good life. He had been a good man and a good Marine.

CHAPTER FOUR
BATTLEFIELD MIRACLES

General Colin Powell's Rules

- It ain't as bad as it looks. It will look beter in the morning.
- Get mad, then get over it.
- Avoid having your ego so close to your position, that when your position falls, your ego goes with it.
- It can be done.
- Be careful what you choose. You may get it.
- Don't let adverse facts stand in the way of a good decision.
- You can't make someone else's choices. You shouldn't let anyone make yours.
- Check small things.
- Share credit.
- Remain kind. Be calm.
- Have a vision. Be demanding.
- Don't take counsel of your fears or naysayers.
- Perpetual optimism is a force multiplier

"It is well that war is so terrible.. else we should grow too fond of it." General Robert E. Lee.

"In every battle there comes a time when both sides consider themselves beaten, then he who continues the attack wins." General Ulysses S. Grant

In October of 1973, during the Yon Kippur War, I was an Army Captain, stationed in Heidelberg, Germany, at the United States Army in Europe Headquarters, at a small installation known as Campbell Barracks. I had been assigned as the Middle East

PLEASE STAND

Desk Officer, and my duties included preparing daily briefings for Officers who usually included at least one General Officer, and keeping a situation map current of whatever was happening in the Middle East. The Yom Kippur War got its name from the fact that five Arab Nations launched an attack on Israel during the solemn feast of Yom Kippur,

When I left that briefing room at the close of the first day of the Yom Kippur War, the map told the awful and grim story of what certainly appeared to be the imminent demise of the Nation of Israel. Israel was illustrated by a small circle, representing the enclave, which almost the entirety of the Israeli Armed Forces occupied. In every direction around the Israeli enclave you could see four huge arrows coming down against the Israelis. Actually, it had begun with five arrows, representing five Arab Nations all opposing Israel. Jordan had been persuaded by the United States to abstain from participating.

During a crisis such as that War, we all worked 12 hour shifts. My shift was ending, and I was tired enough to look forward to getting home and getting some sleep. As I walked out of that room I glanced for a last time at the map and the story the map told was that Israel was finished, about to be annihilated, and that there might not be anything left of the new and fledging State of Israel by the next day.

You might question why I am writing about Israel in a Book about these United States. I begin by writing about Israel because that Nation is unquestionably God's Country, and the citizens of Israel are God's own people. Remember the Scripture. When God gave the Land of Israel to Abraham, He said, "I will bless those that bless thee, and I will curse him who curses you." (Genesis 12:3) Remember back over the life of modern Israel. When nobody wanted to come to Israel's aid, they have always been able to count on the United States as an ally. We are blessed by God on our battlefields, just as Israel has always been blessed by God.

When I walked back into the briefing room the next day, I quickly looked at the Situation map and I was stunned by what I saw. The arrows that had all been descending on the small Israeli enclave were now reversed. All of the arrows which told the story of an Israeli massacre the previous day, illustrated a miraculous breakout, with Israel obviously large and very much in charge, crushing all of her opponents. I remember thinking, "How is that possible? How on earth is that possible? How can that be?"

Only recently have I come to understand how that reversal of fortunes happened, The simple answer is this, "God did it." Let me tell you just a couple of stories that I believe prove that God alone could have and did in fact, save Israel.

A Small group of Israeli soldiers wandered one night out into a minefield. As soon as they realized that they were surrounded by buried mines, they dropped to their bellies and began probing the ground in front of themselves with knives and bayonets, trying to locate the mines. Suddenly one of the Israeli soldiers began to pray out loud. His prayer was answered in seconds by a fierce wind that blew for several minutes. When the wind finally stopped, the Israelis could look down and see that the wind had blown away the dirt covering all of the mines, showing them exactly where the mines had been buried before the mysterious wind came and blew away the dirt which had been concealing the mines.. When the mines became visible the Israelis simply looked down and carefully stepped around the mines and walked out of the minefield.

In another event a small Israeli unit was positioned about half way up a mountain, when they were suddenly attacked by a vastly superior force of Syrian Infantrymen. The Israelis were on the verge of surrendering when suddenly the Syrians began to come forward and lay down their weapons in surrender to the small Israeli Unit.

PLEASE STAND

The Syrians reported that they saw hundreds of huge angels, standing tall with their great wings spread, and they were right behind the Israelis. None of the Israeli troops saw any angels that day, but the Syrians saw them and they had been terrified of them. The Bible said that God could at any time call forth Legions of Angels. (In Matthew 26:53 we read, "Do you think I cannot call on my Father, and He will at once put at my disposal more than 12 legions of angels?" On that day during a battle in Israel, God called forth a couple of hundred of his mighty angels, and they were enough to strike utter terror into the hearts of those Syrian Soldiers that day. No Israelis reported having seen any angels that day. God knew they didn't need to see them.

Now I will tell you a few stories about miracles which have been well documented to have occurred on Battlefields in the United States. For many years the Coat worn in Battle by George Washington was displayed at the Smithsonian Museum in Washington D.C.

George Washington's Coat was penetrated by a bullet leaving a sizable hole just over where the man's heart functioned, Many years after the battle where George Washington received the bullet holes in his jacket he met with an old Indian Chief, who had fought against him during the French and Indian War. The Chief told George Washington, "I shot at you myself several times, and am certain that I hit you on two occasions. After I saw what was happening I spread the word to my men not to shoot at you because you were obviously protected by your God."

Another story concerns a bright sunny Sunday Morning in Boston. People were walking to their churches, enjoying the sunshine and the beautiful day. The Revarand Thomas Prince began to preach, when a commotion arose in the back of his church. Someone had announced that a fleet of 70 French ships was sailing into the harbor, and appeared to be preparing to open fire on Boston. Later the citizens would learn that those ships carried 8,000 troops who were prepared to come ashore and conduct a killing raid on Boston. The master plan of those Frenchmen was to move down the Eastern Coast of America wiping out every city on their route to the South. Suddenly the bell in the church tower began to ring and nobody was in the tower to cause that bell to ring. At least one parishioner reported that the ringing of the bell sounded strange, eerie, just not right. The Reverend Prince raised his arms and began to pray. "We hear thy voice, Oh Lord, We hear it, that breath of yours upon the waters , even upon the deep. The bell tolls for the death of our enemies. There be thy glory, Lord. Amen and amen." Some report that only seconds after Reverend Price finished praying, a massive dark cloud blotted out the bright sunshine, and an awesome wind began to blow. That wind sank many of the French ships and drowned most of the troops onboard. Two commanders of those French vessels committed suicide.

This final story concerns a mysterious fog that covered General Washungton and his troops. George Washington and his troops were terribly outnumbered and his enemy waited throughout the night for just enough daylight to allow them to cross the river in New York, and massacre Washington and his men. When the sun finally did rise it revealed a mysterious fogbank covering the sight of Washington and his small army. While the fog covered Washington and his troops from the view of the vastly superior British Force, Washington's men quietly rowed away, crossing the river under the cover of the fog. When the last boat was leaving General Washington came onboard, and the men slipped away beneath the cover of the fog, As soon as the last boat, carrying Washington and his men, was safely across the river, the fog lifted, as mysteriously as it had appeared. That fog that simply appeared from nowhere, facilitated one of the great escapes in the annals of warfare.

CHAPTER FIVE
THOSE WHO KNEEL

'As a former NFL Player, I am one American who will have nothing to do with any NFL Team that cannot find the corporate courage to stand for the millions of courageous past great Americans whose sacrifice gave meaning to our flag and national anthem." Burgess Owens, former NFL Player

MY DISAGREEMENT

I am a fan of Professional Football, and on several occasions I have paid under $100 to sit in the stands and watch games. As soon as the NFL Players stop this current nonsense of kneeling during the national anthem, I will probably return to a football field and again I will pay to watch my favorite game, a football contest. I totally agree with what Burgess Owens wrote about not wanting any part of disrespecting my Country, its National Anthem or its Flag. I also believe that any citizen who spends even a nickel to watch any NFL game, for as long as this disrespect continues, is showing disrespect for our country.

Meanwhile, I also believe that any young man who has earned an opportunity to play for any team in the NFL should indeed take that opportunity and be paid whatever he NFL will pay him for his participation. Sports Illustrated conducted a study and reported that the average salary for an NFL Offensive lineman, at any position, was $1,267,402. Meanwhile a survey conducted by the National Association of Colleges and Employers (NACE) indicates that the average graduate of a four year college makes about $50,000 a year. For an employee making about $50,000 a year to earn over a million dollars would take about 20 years.

During one study, during the 35 year period between 1959 and 1988, 517 former NFL Players died at an average age of 59.6 years, compared to 431 deaths among Major League Baseball players who died at an average age of 66.7 years.

I found this information on the life expectancy of NFL Players at NFLdiamonds.com-/2015/005/NFLplayers-life-expectancy/

I had lived in Sherman, Texas for several years in 1979, during which time I served as the President of the local chapter of the American Heart Association. Each year we conducted a fund raiser in the form of a bike-a-thon. A local gentleman named Vernon Holland had played offensive tackle for the Cincinnati Bengals. He played the last game of his career one Sunday afternoon in Dallas, against the Cowboys. After the game he celebrated the fact that he had spent most of the afternoon keeping one of the Cowboys, called "Too Tall" Jones out of the Cincinnati Backfield. He celebrated by going on a local radio station and inviting anyone who wanted to come, to join him for drinks at the local Holiday Inn.

Vern was somewhat of a celebrity, and I always invited him when he was in town, to come to the Heart Association fund raisers because he always helped to pull in crowds. Vern often came to our events wearing shorts and a tank top. His clothing revealed long surgical scars on each of his knees and each of his shoulders. Vern had paid an expensive price for the many years he had played the game of football. Very expensive.

Sadly, on April 20, 1988, Vern Holland died at the age of 49, Vern died at the Nashville Memorial Hospital after suffering a heart attack at his home. Vern was a good man, and the world was a better place because he had been part of it. I talk about you often, dear friend, and we all still miss you. I'll bet that fellow they called "Too Tall" remembers you also.

I included some of what I know about Vern Holland for two very important reasons. I told you about the scars on his body because I want you to understand that playing professional football is painful. Every practice session and every game can cause you a lot of pain. Yes, you can indeed make a lot of money playing in the NFL, but never make the mistake of believing that playing football is easy money. I can't think of any of those jobs where college graduates qualify for that pays close to $50,000 a year, where it is probable where you will. during your career, be hurt so severely that you will require surgery. The second reason I wrote about Vern Holland is that I want you to realize that playing in the NFL can, and almost surly will, shorten your life. As I have already mentioned NFL Players can make a lot of money, but that money never comes easily, and in the long run it can kill you.

WHAT FORMER PRESIDENT TRUMP SAID ABOUT KNEELING DURING THE NATIONAL ANTHEM

In a campaign speech in Alabama, Former President Donald Trump said that players who kneel should be fired. The Former President said. "Wouldn't you love to see one of these NFL owners, when somebody disrespects our flag, to say, 'get that son of a bitch off the field right now. Out! He's fired. He's fired." Imagine that. He is a man who has made a gazillion dollars, and actually got himself elected to the Presidency of the United States, and he manages to foul up a simple message, by referring to NFL Players who kneel as "s.o.b.'s" With all that man knows about so many things you would think he would be smart enough to get someone to check his speeches and his casual tweets and online comments and help him avoid making colossal and stupid mistakes such as referring to some NFL Players as "s.o.b.'s." I believe it is silliness like that, which cost Mr. Trump the last election. I strongly agree that kneeling NFL players deserve to be fired, but I would never, ever, under any circumstances I can imagine, call any one of them an "s.o.b." That just isn't any way a gentleman should talk, Not ever, under any circumstances. Its just wrong, and I know it, and nobody has ever called me brilliant. The truth is that my Mom and Dad taught me better than that.

NOW ITS MY TURN TO TALK

When the War in Viet Nam broke out, I was a typical Alabama redneck and could hardly wait to get there and fight with some part of the United States Armed Forces. That is just the way we rednecks were raised and taught. I got over to Fort Benning as fast as I could, where they allowed me to have free training at the United States Army Airborne and Ranger Schools. I had heard that the First Cavalry Division would be one of the first units to go and fight, so I signed up with those men. Sure enough, they gave me free passage on a ship named the USS Buckner, and that ship sailed all the way across the Pacific Ocean to drop me off with a couple of hundred of my new friends, on the Shores of Viet Nam in a city called Qui Nohn. I served under the best Battalion Commander who ever lived, Lieutenant Colonel Robert B. Tully. I also was blessed to have the best Platoon Sergeant in the Army, Sergeant First Class Rogilio Salinas. Sergeant Salinas spent eight years training young men at the Army's Ranger School. Sgt Salinas recently retired as a Sergeant Major.

I was deeply honored by Lieutenant Colonel Tully to be appointed by him to lead the Reconnaissance Platoon in the second of the fifth infantry battalion, and to get to lead that platoon in Viet Nam.. A few weeks after I began to lead the Recon Platoon I was privileged to be allowed to fight in the IA Drang Valley on a landing zone we called LZ X-Ray.

In 1968 I was a Captain, and they allowed me to go back to Viet Nam and to serve as an advisor to the Phoenix Program under the very able leadership of the CIA. I mention these experiences because I believe they qualify me to comment on respect for the National Anthem, my Flag and my Country. Here are my capsular comments.

" I have deep respect for any American Citizen who has the gumption to peacefully protest for a just cause. That is a right and privilege guaranteed to every American by our Constitution. I have absolutely no problem with any NFL Player protesting a just cause. What does offend me deeply is not what is being protested but I detest WHEN it is happening. I believe the National Anthem is one of the sacred rituals we as a Nation have chosen to honor the estimated 1.1 million men and women who have given their greatest possession, their very lives, in defense of our great and totally unique Nation. To do absolutely anything but stand erect with your hand over your heart, during the playing of the National Anthem, is irreverent, inappropriate and just downright wrong. It should cease immediately, because it is so grossly uncouth and wrong."

In addition to what I have written in this book, I have designed a t-shirt with white lettering on red cloth that reads,

BOYCOTT THE NFL

UNTIL

EVERY MAN STANDS

You are welcomed to buy one or more of these t-shirts at my website found at www.pleasestand.com.

FRANCIS SCOTT KEY WAS A JERK, BUT BOY-HOWDY COULD HE EVER WRITE A POEM !

Francis Scott Key owned black slaves. He also said some really horrible things about black people. Francis Scott Key was probably, based on the two things I just reported, a world-class jerk. Francis Scott Key was also a very gifted poet who wrote five beautiful stanzas to a poem titled The Star Spangled Banner, which was soon put to music. Mr. Key, as all human beings are, was capable of doing some despicable things and in the very same life time he did some great and beautiful things.

Let me present an example that illustrates my point about people being capable of both very bad or evil things, and also being capable of doing grand and beautiful things. I know almost nothing about his personal life, but only for the purpose of this example, let us assume for a minute that author Ernst Hemmingway was a jerk and lived a life that almost nobody could or would admire. Remember, I have no idea if that was true or false, however, even if it was true, the old man could still deliver remarkable stories in the books he wrote.

It is an error in logic to believe that The Star Spangled Banner is flawed, because in some and possibly many areas, it's author was so deeply flawed. It really doesn't work that way. Our National Anthem is a beautiful and thought provoking song about, "the land of the free and the home of the brave."

CHAPTER SIX
ARE YOU WORTHY?

"Live simply so others may simply live," Mother Teresa

"A great many people (not you) do now seem to think that the mere state of being worried is in itself meritorious. I don't think it is. We must, if it so happens, give our lives for others; but even while we're doing it, I think we're meant to enjoy Our Lord, and, in Him, our friends, our food, our sleep, our jokes, and the bird's song and the frosty sunrise." C.S. Lewis

"For God so loved the world that He gave His one and only Son," John 3:16, NIV

HOW TO BE WORTHY

Last night I watched one of my favorite movies, "Saving Private Ryan," for the 2d time. That movie does two things very well. It depicts the sheer horror of combat, and it asks a question of the Character, Private Ryan, that, I believe, we should all be able to answer. The question comes when the Captain (Portrayed by Tom Hanks) leading the rescue mission of Private Ryan is dying of a combat wound. The Captain, known as Captain Miller, is dying in a street, when he calls Private Ryan to hear his last words. Captain Miller had just completed a rescue mission of Private Ryan, and he lost several men during that search, including his own and the life of his First Sergeant. In the Movie, the Captain Miller Character, challenges Private Ryan to live his life so that he will be worthy of the lives lost during his rescue.

My question, which reveals my greatest reason for writing this small Book, is to ask you the same question that Captain Miller asked Private Ryan in the movie. Has your life been worthy of the men who died for you?

The greatest and most significant death anyone ever died for you, was the death of Jesus Christ on His cross on Mount Calvary. Any understanding of that crucifixion must begin with an understanding that the cruel and vicious murder of Jesus Christ was intended, by God Himself, to be personal, an act He performed for you, just as if you were the only living person on Earth.

In what is probably the most frequently recited verse of the entire Bible, in John 3:16. we read, "For God so loved the world that He gave His one and only Son..." Let's take a quick look at the word, "World," in that verse. "World" in this verse has nothing to do with geography. God is not admiring His own handiwork, in His snow capped mountains, or His pristine rivers and lakes. In this verse, the word, "World," comes from the Greek word, "kosmos," which is translated into the English word, "mankind," God sent Jesus, His only son, to die for you and for every human being, so that He could bear punishment for all of the sins which we could never repay. Now, think about the enormity of what Jesus did for you, and ask yourself the same question Private Ryan was asked in the Movie: are you worthy? Are you, in any way, worthy of what Jesus did for you?

Now ask yourself if you are worthy of any single one of the deaths of the 1.1 million men and women who gave their lives so you might live and enjoy life as a citizen of this great nation? Men and women shoulder weapons and march determinedly into battle, sometimes almost surly knowing that they will not survive. They do that for you, because they love you. You can't prepare yourself

PLEASE STAND

for the hell on earth which is combat by hating. Hating Hitler was not enough to push those men forward at Normandy. It was a good start, but what really got them going was not hatred, but love, love of country, which easily translates into loving Americans.

Don't you dare even think about kneeling and disrespecting a single one of the 1.1 million who gave absolutely everything, including their very lives, so that you might hold your head high as a certified citizen of the Land of the Free and the Home of the Brave. Put this all into perspective by realizing that you are not insulting one or two service members. You are insulting and essentially trashing the memory of 1,1 million men and women who gave their very lives for you. Make it personal because it is personal. Those good men and women died so that you might live free.

Appreciate what is represented here, by imagining a huge stadium, with 100,000 seats, with every single seat occupied. Now imagine 11 packed stadiums like that in a row, with each one packed to capacity. That is about `1.1 million people. Now, imagine every one of the people in those stadiums as a dead body stacked high on a long field. That, dear reader, is precisely what we are talking about when we mention the price 1,1 million men and women have already paid for you and your freedom. You need to stop the silliness right now. If you want to protest then do it at mid-field after the first score, or during half time. If you simply don't get it, and absolutely cannot comprehend why we owe honor to our National Anthem and to our flag, then God help us all. Stand with honor for only one reason; It's the right thing to do.

Chapter Seven
What Is Your Legacy?

"Carve you name on hearts, not tombstones. A Legacy is etched into the minds of others and the stories they share about you." Shannon L. Adler

"We all die. The goal isn't to live foever. The goal is to create something that will." Chuck Palahnik

"Immortality is to live your life dojng good things, and leaving your mark behind." Brandon Lee

When I heard that Burt Reynolds had died I immediately began to wonder what his legacy had been. What did Burt Reynolds do that was unique to life on Planet Earth. My mind immediately went to his college football Career. I have seen a couple of clips of Burt Reynolds carrying a football when he played in College for Florida State. Those clips revealed an amazing running ability that young Mr. Reynolds displayed often as a college football player. I can close my eyes now and see that man running around and away from his opponents. He had extraordinary talent.

Then I began to wonder what I had left to the world. My mind immediately flashed back to my homecoming game of my senior year in high school. I sacked the quarterback on three successive plays and then on fourth and forty, I blocked the kick and fell on the football. That is so very trivial, if after 80 years on this planet, the thing I remember the most occurred at a high school football game. In my defense I will remind my readers that there is something very impressive to a 17 year old kid about 5,000 people at Rickwood Field going insane over something that kid had just achieved. I am sure that about half of those people didn't even know what I had done. Another consideration is that if I have lived 80 years and the most memorable thing I can think of happened in a high school football game, that, in itself, is worse than sad; it is pathetic.

Soon I began to think about how could I change my legacy. The answer came to me very quickly. The most important thing a human being does during his or her entire lifetime is to convince God Almighty that he or she belongs in Heaven and certainly not spending eternity in Hell. Then I thought about how I just might be able to convince one or two fellow travellers on Earth, that they could and absolutely should spend eternity in Heaven with God, and absolutely not forever in Hell.

The next thing I thought about was that I am indeed 80 years old, and I don't have all the time in the world to see my legacy come to life. Then I saw a quotation from David Jeremiah and I believed the wisdom of what he said. He said, "<u>A man of God doing the will of God is immortal until his work is done.</u>" So, there it is. I have all the time I need to help at least one person get to Heaven. ALL I have to do is to write or speak something that will be heard by at least one soul, that gives them specific instruction on how to get to Heaven.

How to Get to Heaven

Absolutely everything you will ever need to get to Heaven you can get from Acts 16, and you only need to remember ten words from that entire Chapter, because those ten words contain all the information you will ever need to spend eternity with Jesus Christ, in Heaven. I'll begin this story by telling you that it was about midnight, and that Paul and Silas were in prison, with their feet in stocks. Now what do you imagine these two great men of God were doing at about midnight?

They were praying and singing songs to God. Would you expect these great men of God to be cursing their fortune and their jailers? Not a chance. They were singing hymns and praying. Well, obviously, God wanted to move this story along so about midnight he sent an "great earthquake," so the very foundations of the prison were shaken, and all the doors to the cells were thrown open. The jailer woke up and saw that all the doors were opened, so he drew his sword, and was about to kill himself, for allowing all of his prisoners to escape. No death could be as terrible as the humiliating death of an old soldier who had failed his mission so miserably. Just as the jailer was about to fall on his own sword, Paul called out to him, shouting, "Do not harm yourself, for we are all here."

That jailer must have been as surprised as he had ever been during his entire lifetime. He called for a torch and came into the cell of Paul and Silas. Then he brought them out of their cells and into the light. Then he asked the most important question any man could ever ask. He cried out, "Sirs, what must I do to be saved?" Paul and Silas replied, with ten words that tells the complete story of salvation. They said, "Believe in the Lord Jesus, and you will be saved."

Now I am going to tell you how you can even shorten the message from Paul and Silas. If you want to get to heaven, to live forever with Jesus, just do this one thing, "BELIEVE!" That's it boys and girls! You get to heaven when you believe. Read the first five words of the Bible and realize why it is very close to impossible to not believe. "In the beginning God created…" That's it, readers. The God who created every nuance and intricacy of the entire universe must be God, for God alone could manage such a task as that.

All you have to do to participate in forever, with that generous and gracious God is "BELIEVE!"

I recently heard a preacher say something I consider brilliant. He said "Hell is not filled with people who have sinned." The Bible says "For all have sinned," and Hell just doesn't have the room for all of us. I also heard a Preacher say "Hell isn't filled with sinners. It's filled with non-believers."

My final words in this Chapter are for those who aren't there yet, and still have trouble believing. Like every thing else in life, God is always standing by, and He is ready to answer your prayers. If you don't have faith yet, then ask God for it. Faith is a gift and God can arrange a special delivery for you. Go ahead! Just ask Him! See what happens.

Chapter Eight
WATCH YOUR MOUTH!

"I had three rules for my players: No Profanity, Don't criticize a teammate. Never be late." John Wooden,

This is the text of a General Order issued by General George Washington as he spoke out against profanity.

"General Orders, August 3, 1776."

"The General is sorry to be informed that the foolish and wicked practice of profane cursing and swearing, a vice hitherto little known in our American Army is growing into fashion. He hopes that the officers will, by example, as well as influence, endeavor to check it and that both they and the men will reflect that we can little hope of the blessing of Heaven on our army if we insult it by our impiety and folly. Added to this is a vice so mean and low without any temptation that every man of sense and character detests and despises it." Signed by George Washington, General and Commander, United States Army.

Unqualified to Coach

I recently watched a TV program about men who coach pee-wee football teams. I was saddened and disappointed when I heard those coaches letting fly with profanities, obscenities and blasphemies in front of the children they were trying to coach. That, dear readers, is nonsense, baloney and a serious mistake about what it takes to coach young men and young women. It doesn't take a genius to be able to teach these young people how to demonstrate the fundamentals and display a working knowledge of the strategies behind the execution of the games they are coaching. What definitely is required is an understanding of and an appreciation for the sacred code of conduct required by adults who would attempt to lead and teach young people.

Please pay close attention to every word in this next sentence. If you are teaching or coaching those precious young boys and girls, require and demand more than you are capable of providing right now. So do the right thing and stay far away from children until you are willing and able to set an example that will make them better men, or women. Then make certain that you are capable and willing to work for those young people, at a two hour practice or a game. If you cannot, or will not, master that self discipline, to accomplish that without cursing, swearing or using blasphemies, please go immediately and resign your coaching or teaching position, because you are incapable of presenting the example required to lead or teach young people. Until you are willing and capable of presenting at least an adequate example of adult leadership, then you know better than to continue to daily demonstrate the message of. "This is not how a gentleman does it...... but listen and obey me anyway." Baloney again, and you know, down deep in your heart the truth. As the tired old cliché communicates so accurately "Shape up or ship out." You know the right thing, now just do it.

If you are coaching older and more mature men or women, then stop the nonsense of telling yourself and others a load of this nonsense about avoiding obscenities is not for older, more mature people. This isn't something you teach to grown-ups. Again, Baloney! Look again at the first quotation I showed you to begin this chapter. John Wooden, possibly the greatest all around College Basketball Coach ever, said that he only had 3 rules. Rule 1 was, "No profanity." Clear enough? Do you think that possibly that was his number one rule because it was important to him? What do you think? Is it important to you? What do you think?

www.ingramcontent.com/pod-product-compliance
Lightning Source LLC
LaVergne TN
LVHW040200080526
838202LV00042B/3258